PETER PAN

PETER PAN

JAMES M. BARRIE

Retold by
Susan Shebar

Illustrated by
T. Lewis

Troll Associates

Library of Congress Cataloging in Publication Data

Shebar, Susan E.
    Peter Pan.

    Summary: The adventures of the three Darling
children in Neverland with Peter Pan, the boy who
would not grow up.
    [1. Fantasy] I. Barrie, J.M. (James Matthew),
1860-1937. Peter Pan. II. Lewis, T. (Thomas), ill.
III. Title.
PZ7.S53814Pe   1988   [Fic]   87-15480
ISBN 0-8167-1199-2 (lib. bdg.)
ISBN 0-8167-1200-X (pbk.)

Wendy, John, and Michael Darling were fast asleep in their bedroom. Their parents had already left for a party. Nana, the family dog, slept near the garden in the yard. All was quiet in the Darling house this night.

Suddenly, the bedroom lights blinked, then went out. An instant later, another light shone in the room. It was a small, brilliant light—a hundred times stronger than regular light.

The tiny light dashed about the room, then came to rest. Moments later, the window blew open wide. A boy dropped through it into the room. He was dressed in green with leaves for a shirt. The tiny light dashed past the boy, flew about the room, and then disappeared inside a jug.

"Tinker Bell," the boy called softly. "Do come out and help me look for my shadow."

A tiny tinkle of golden bells flowed up from the jug. For the light inside the jug was not a light at all. It was a fairy no bigger than your hand.

Tinker Bell flew out of the jug and sat on the big chest. The boy jumped onto the chest too. When he did, something came tumbling out of one of the drawers. There on the floor lay the boy's shadow. The boy whooped with delight. He was so excited that he slammed the chest drawer closed, trapping Tinker Bell inside.

The boy stepped on his shadow, thinking it would stick to him. But it did not stick. When he saw a bar of soap on the wash basin, he grabbed it, rubbing it on his feet. Then he stood up and stepped on his shadow again. It still would not stick. He stamped his foot and began to cry. His sobs woke Wendy. She sat up.

"Who are you?" Wendy asked, clearly startled.

The boy rose to his feet and bowed politely. "I am Peter Pan, and I have come for my shadow."

"Well," Wendy said slowly, "you can't put your shadow on that way. I guess I could sew it on for you."

As Wendy sewed, Peter Pan told her how he had come to lose his shadow.

"I often visit this room," he said. "I sit in the open window and listen to your mother when she tells her wonderful stories. But one night, after you and the boys were asleep, your mother saw me. I flew away, but my shadow caught on a nail and tore off."

"There—all finished," Wendy said, snipping the last bit of string from the shadow. "You shouldn't be peeking in people's windows, you know. Besides, doesn't your mother tell you stories?"

Peter stood and lifted his foot. His shadow sprang to life. It was still a bit wrinkled, but it did everything Peter did.

"I don't have a mother," he said.

"No mother?" Wendy asked sadly. "Then how do you live? Where do you live?"

"Second star to the right," Peter said. He was pointing out the window. "And I'm all right. I ran away when I heard my mother and father talking about what I should be when I grew up. I never want to grow up. I want to stay a boy and have fun. So now I live in Neverland with the Lost Boys."

Just then, Peter noticed Tinker Bell was missing. Where was she? He sprang to the top of the chest. "Tink, are you in there? Come out and meet Wendy."

The drawer shook, and there was a faint tinkle of bells. But the fairy would not come out. She did not like the attention Peter was giving Wendy.

Wendy was delighted. "Peter," she cried, "you don't mean to tell me there is a fairy in this room!"

Peter pulled the drawer open and Tinker Bell flew out. She brushed past Peter's hand. Fairy dust sprinkled across his fingers. Wendy had to bend down to get out of Tinker Bell's way.

"Peter, who are the Lost Boys?" Wendy asked.

"They are the boys who fell out of their baby carriages when their parents were looking the other way. If they are not claimed in seven days, they are sent to Neverland. I am their captain."

"What fun it must be!"

"Yes," said Peter. "But we are lonely too. And we have no one to tell us stories." Then Peter had an idea. "Wendy, do come with us and tell stories to the Lost Boys, Tink, and me."

"Oh, I can't," Wendy said quickly. "Think of my brother John and baby Michael."

Peter scratched his head, then he brightened. "Bring them too," he said.

"But Peter, I can't fly."

"I'll teach you! It's easy," Peter said.

"Will you teach John and Michael too?"

"Of course," Peter said. He sprang into the air.

Wendy ran to John and Michael to wake them.

"Wake up!" she cried. "Peter Pan has come. He's going to teach us to fly!"

John rubbed his eyes and sat up. "I say, Peter, can you really fly?"

Peter flew around the room.

"Wow!" said Michael.

"Your turn," Peter said.

The three children jumped on their beds, spread their arms, and tried to fly. But they all went down instead of up.

Peter laughed. "No, no," he said.

"How do you do it?" John asked, rubbing his knees.

"Think lovely thoughts, and the thoughts will lift you into the air."

The children tried again. Each thought the loveliest thought they could think. But not one of them started to fly. Peter scratched his head again. Then he remembered. No one can fly without fairy dust. Peter still

had Tinker Bell's fairy dust on his fingers. He clapped his hands in delight, then sprinkled each of the children with a bit of it.

"Now, think lovely thoughts and wiggle your shoulders this way," he said, wiggling his. "And let go."

Michael was the first to try. He thought of large ice-cream cones and wiggled his shoulders. All at once he was in the air. John thought of slaying a fierce dragon. Suddenly, he was in the air also. Wendy closed her eyes. She thought how lovely it would be to fly. When she opened her eyes, she was nearly on the ceiling!

"Look at us!" they cried. Up and down and around they went, swooping, gliding, and giggling.

11

"And now," Peter said, "are you ready to come with me to meet the Lost Boys of Neverland?"

John and Michael looked at Wendy. She was the oldest of the Darling children. She made all of the important decisions.

"Do let's go, Wendy. Please!" John pleaded. "It does sound like fun."

"Yes, yes, I want to go too," Michael added. Wendy hesitated. Peter hopped onto the windowsill.

"There are mermaids," he said. "And pirates."

"Pirates! Let's go at once!" John cried.

It was just at that moment that Mr. and Mrs. Darling returned home from the party. They would have reached the bedroom in time to stop the children if it had not been for Tinker Bell. She warned Peter to be quick. Peter called to the children.

"Not a moment to lose!" He soared out into the starlit sky with Tinker Bell, Wendy, John, and Michael close behind. Their dog, Nana, woke in time to see the children fly out of the window. She yelped and barked at the children, but they did not hear her as they flew away into the night.

"Second star to the right and straight on till morning," Peter said, urging them on.

The children flew the whole night, through the dark heavens and the wispy clouds. They weaved in and out of the twinkling stars.

Early in the morning the children could see whales far below in the sea. Peter flew down and rode on a whale's back. The whale spouted water through his blowhole. The children laughed and Peter splashed in the spray.

Michael had begun to grow tired and fell asleep. Down he dropped toward the cold, dark sea. Peter laughed. But Wendy was afraid. "Save him!" she cried.

Peter stopped laughing. He dove down through the air toward the falling baby. Michael had almost reached the water when Peter swooped under him and lifted him up. Michael woke with a start.

"There it is, Neverland at last!" said Peter, pointing ahead. "Just follow the arrows."

The children looked all around. A million golden arrows glittered above their heads. They all pointed toward the island called Neverland. Wendy could see beautiful mermaids swimming in the bay. Soon the arrows faded, however. A gloomy mist covered part of the island where a ship sat in the water.

Peter turned toward the children. "There are pirates asleep on the ship below us. If you like, we can go down and fight them."

John grew very excited. "I say, who is their captain?" he asked.

"Hook," Peter answered. His face grew stern. He hated Captain James Hook.

"What is he like? Is he big?"

"Well, he is not as big as he once was," Peter said proudly. "I cut off his hand and threw it in the sea. It was eaten by a crocodile."

"Oh, my," John said, quite amazed. "Then he can't fight now?"

"Oh, can he ever!" Peter said. "He has an iron hook instead of a right hand. He uses it like a claw." Peter grew serious. "There is one thing that every boy who serves under me must promise. If we meet Hook in an open fight, you must leave him to me."

The boys quickly agreed. They shook hands. Peter turned to face the bay below and began to fly down toward it. Peter did not know that some of the pirates were still awake. They had seen him in the sky and had pointed their big gun, Long Tom, up at him. Suddenly, the cannon blasted. The shot missed. But the exploding force of air blew Peter, John and Michael far out to sea. Wendy and Tinker Bell were blown upward. The two became separated from the others.

Tinker Bell flew back and forth close to Wendy. Her tiny bell tinkled and fairy dust filled the air. Wendy thought Tinker Bell was her friend, so she followed the fairy's lead. But Tinker Bell was jealous of Wendy. She was trying to think of a way to get rid of the girl.

15

Far below, in Neverland, the Lost Boys heard the sound of Long Tom. They knew that Captain Hook used the gun only on Peter Pan. And so the six Lost Boys went out looking for Peter. First, there was Tootles. He had a sweet, kind nature. Nibs was happy and lighthearted, while Slightly thought a great deal of himself. Curly was always in some sort of trouble. And the twins stayed close together.

The Indians who lived on the island were also loyal to Peter Pan. Peter had once saved their princess, Tiger Lily, from the evil pirates. When the Indians heard the big gun, they went out searching for the pirates. The pirates, in turn, were out searching for the Lost Boys. Everyone was circling the island. But no one met because they were all going the same way at the same time.

Suddenly, the Lost Boys heard the pirates approach from a distance. As fast as they could, the Lost Boys ran through the forest to the seven largest trees. Each one had a hole big enough for any of the boys or Peter to slip through. The holes were entrances to the underground home Peter and the Lost Boys shared. Quickly, then, the six Lost Boys disappeared down the tree holes. But before they did, a pirate saw Nibs running through the woods.

"Shall I go after him, Captain?" he asked.

"Not now," Hook said. "I want to catch the six of them and their leader too. Fan out and look for them all."

The pirates were a mean gang. And none was meaner among them than Captain Hook. He was tall and thin. His hair hung in long, dark curls. And instead of a right hand, he had an iron hook with a very sharp point.

Hook turned to the pirate he trusted most, Smee. Hook talked about Peter Pan.

" 'Twas he who cut off my hand, Smee, and flung it to a crocodile. That crocodile liked the taste of my hand. He has been following me ever since, licking his lips. Now he's waiting to eat the rest of me."

Hook sat on a mushroom. He took a deep breath and sighed. There was a quiver in his voice.

"Smee," he said, "that crocodile would have had me before now. But by a lucky chance it swallowed a clock that goes tick-tick inside it. Whenever it comes close, I hear the tick and run away."

"Someday," said Smee, "the clock will run down, and then he will get you."

Hook wetted his lips. "Aye," he said. "That's the fear that haunts me."

Hook's seat began to feel warm. He stood up. "Smee, this mushroom is hot."

Hook and Smee looked carefully at the huge mushroom. There was something strange about it. They stretched their arms around the mushroom and pulled hard. It popped out of the ground with a jolt. Stranger still, smoke began to pour out of the hole in the ground. The pirates looked at each other.

"A chimney!" they both exclaimed. Hook put his ear close to the chimney. He could hear children's voices.

"Smee, it's the Lost Boys," Hook whispered.

All the pirates returned to listen. Then they replaced the mushroom. Hook stood for a long time, thinking.

"Return to the ship," he said at last to his men. "Bake a large rich cake. Make it chocolate with green sugar on it. We will bring it back here where the boys will find it. They will gobble it up because they do not have a mother to tell them that too much cake will make them sick. Then we will catch them!" All the pirates burst into laughter.

Through their laughter, however, they could hear a small sound. It came from the stream in the forest. It moved closer toward the mushroom chimney, closer toward the pirates, closer toward Captain Hook. *Tick-tick-tick-tick!* Hook turned pale and trembled. His teeth began to rattle in his mouth.

"The crocodile!" he gasped. Hook turned and ran as fast as he could out of the woods and to his waiting ship.

Not long after the pirates left, the Lost Boys decided to search for Peter Pan again. They began to spread out in all directions. But Nibs called them back together.

"Hurry," he called. "I have seen a great bird. It is flying this way. And as it flies, it calls 'Poor Wendy!' It must be a Wendy bird!"

The boys were very excited. They had never seen a Wendy bird. Tinker Bell flew down among the boys. She had a plan.

"Peter wants you to shoot the Wendy bird," she said.

The boys looked at each other. They never questioned their captain's orders. Tootles had a bow and arrow with him. He took out the arrow and placed it on the bow. He drew the string back, then stopped.

Tinker Bell could hardly wait.

"Quick, Tootles, quick!" she screamed. "Peter will be so pleased."

"Out of the way," Tootles shouted. He fired. The arrow soared into the air and struck Wendy in her chest. Wendy fluttered and fell onto the hard ground. She lay very still.

Tinker Bell flew over the boys. She laughed, then flew into the forest to hide. The boys crowded around Wendy.

Soon they heard Peter calling to them.

"Great news, boys," he cried. "At last I have brought a mother for you all. Her name is Wendy. Have you seen her? I believe she flew this way."

The boys looked stricken.

"Peter," Tootles said slowly, "a terrible thing has happened, and we are very sorry."

They stood back. Peter saw Wendy lying on the ground. John and Michael began to cry.

"Whose arrow?" Peter asked sternly.

Tootles fell to his knees. "Mine, Peter," he said.

Peter pulled the arrow out of Wendy's chest. He raised it above Tootles, holding it like a dagger. Tootles did not move.

"Strike, Peter," he said.

"I cannot strike," Peter said. "Something is holding my arm back."

Suddenly, Nibs cried out, "Look! It's Wendy! Wendy is alive!"

Wendy smiled up at Peter. Peter bent down. Carefully, he lifted Wendy into his arms and carried her into his underground home. For the next several days, Peter, the Lost Boys, John, and Michael nursed Wendy back to health.

Wendy, John, and Michael loved the underground home. It had one large room with a dirt floor. Growing up from it were large mushrooms that the boys used as stools. A fireplace warmed the room. One bed stood against the back wall.

At six-thirty every night, Wendy pulled the bed down. It almost filled the room. All of the boys would hop onto the bed. Wendy would tell stories until they fell asleep.

Tinker Bell had finally come home. She was very sorry for what she had tried to do to Wendy. Wendy understood and forgave her.

One night, Wendy settled down to tell a story. Michael, John, and the Lost Boys were in bed. Peter sat on a mushroom stool with Tinker Bell on his shoulder. As Wendy prepared to tell her story, pirates crept through the woods above. They wanted to catch the Indians. Slowly, they circled the Indian village and waited for the sign to attack.

"There was once a gentleman and a lady," Wendy began. "Their names were Mr. and Mrs. Darling. They had three children—John, Michael, and Wendy. They had a dog named Nana. One night, Peter Pan flew into their house. He taught the children how to fly. And he told them about the Lost Boys in Neverland."

The boys in the bed smiled.

"The children wanted to meet the Lost Boys. So, Peter, Tink, and the children flew away to Neverland."

Now came the part Peter hated.

"The children knew their mother and father would always keep the window open for them to fly back,"continued Wendy. "And so the children stayed in Neverland for many years and had a happy time."

Peter could stand no more of the story. He jumped up and stamped his feet.

"A lot you know about mothers," he said. "I thought my mother would always keep the window open for me too. But when I tried to go home, I found the window was closed and locked. There was another boy sleeping in my bed. I couldn't go home again, not ever."

Wendy, John and Michael grew afraid.

"We must go home at once," Wendy said. "Peter, will you make the arrangements?"

Peter was surprised, then angry. He didn't know his words would make the children leave. He didn't want Wendy to go home.

"No, I won't," he said coldly.

Wendy looked hurt. Peter felt sorry for her.

"Tinker Bell can take you across the sea if you really want to do it," he said slowly.

Wendy looked at the Lost Boys. They were sad to be losing their only mother.

"If you will all come to our home, I'm sure my father and mother will let you live with us," she said.

The Lost Boys jumped for joy. "Peter, can we go?"

"All right," Peter said with a bitter voice. "But I will not go with you. I'm going to stay in Neverland. I never want to grow up. I'm going to stay a boy and have fun."

Wendy and the boys begged Peter to go with them. But he refused.

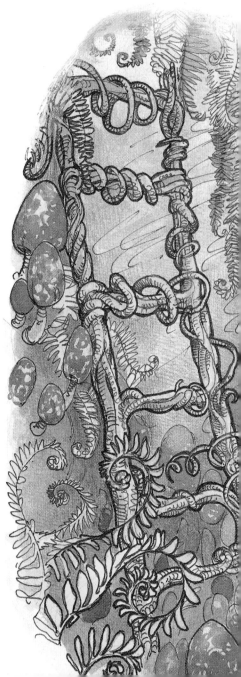

"It's all right," Wendy said at last. "Peter knows the way to the window. He can come whenever he wishes to see us again."

Tinker Bell and the children gathered their things for the trip. One by one they said good bye to Peter. They each made their way up through the hole to the ground above their home.

All of a sudden, loud shouts and cries filled the air. The children rushed back underground.

"Peter, what is it?" Wendy asked. The noise had frightened them.

"The pirates have attacked the Indians!" Peter said. "Everyone stay quiet, and listen. If the Indians have won, they will beat the tom-tom. That's always their victory signal."

Above ground, the pirates' attack took the Indians by surprise. Most of the tribe was captured. Princess Tiger Lily and a few Indian braves escaped through the dark woods.

Smee searched the Chief's tepee until he found the tom-tom. Captain Hook was delighted. He and Smee crept quietly through the forest to the mushroom chimney. Smee beat the tom-tom twice, then stopped to listen. They both pressed their ears close to the chimney.

Down below the boys heard the sound of the drum. "The Indians have won!" Peter shouted.

The children cheered. It would now be safe to leave for home.

Hook signaled to his men. The pirates quickly surrounded the seven trees where Wendy and the boys would come up out of their underground home.

"Think of it, Smee," whispered Hook. "We'll get them all, and we didn't have to give them a cake."

The first to come out of a tree was Curly. He poked his head out of the tree hole and looked around. All of a sudden, a huge pirate clamped his hand over Curly's mouth. A second pirate picked him up and threw him to another, who tossed him to another, until Curly landed on the ground at Hook's feet. Nibs was captured next, then Slightly, then Tootles, and then the twins.

John was the first of the Darling children to come above ground. He too was captured and waited helplessly for Michael to join him.

Wendy was the last to be captured. Hook took off his hat and bowed to her. She tried to scream and warn Peter, but Smee clamped his hand tightly over her mouth. Just then, music from Peter's pipes started to come up through the hole in the tree.

"You see, my dear," Hook sneered, "Peter has forgotten you already."

Wendy tried to bite Smee's hand, but he was too strong for her. Hook laughed and ordered his men to take the captives to his pirate ship. Then Hook rushed to the mushroom chimney and looked inside.

Below ground, Peter played on his pipes. He tried to make believe that he did not care about Wendy and the boys. But he felt so sad and lonely that his head began to hurt. Peter took a bottle of medicine from a shelf. He poured a bit of it into a glass. But he hated to take medicine, so he put it down. At last, he lay down on the bed and forced himself to sleep.

When Hook was sure that Peter was asleep, he lowered himself through the hole and into the underground

house. Silently, he tiptoed to the sleeping Peter Pan. Then he caught sight of the medicine glass and reached into the pocket of his coat for a small vial of black liquid. Hook pulled out the cork and poured five drops from the vial into Peter's glass. He took one long, gloating look at Peter, then slinked back up the tree.

Peter slept for a long time. Just as he was starting to awaken, he heard a small tinkle of bells. "Hi, Tink," he said lazily. "You finally have what you always wanted, Tink. You and I are alone in Neverland."

Tink began to fly wildly around the room. Peter watched and listened carefully as Tinker Bell told him about the capture of Wendy and the boys.

Peter sprang to his feet, grabbing his weapons. He dashed toward the hole that would lead him above ground. But the medicine glass caught Peter's eyes. "Just a minute, Tink," he said. "I'd better drink this first."

"No!" Tink rang her bells loudly. She had overheard Hook talking about his deed. "Something is wrong," she said.

"Don't be silly, Tink. What could be wrong?" He raised the glass to his lips.

Tink panicked. With lightning speed she flew between Peter's lips. When he tipped the glass, Tink drank the medicine before it could reach Peter's mouth. A few moments later, her body began to shake. With Peter's help, she flew to the bed and lay down.

"It was poisoned, Peter." Her voice was growing weak.

Peter knelt beside her. "Oh, Tink!" he cried. "Think beautiful thoughts and the thoughts will help you."

But Tinker Bell's light was growing dimmer. Peter tried shaking her. But it didn't help. He was afraid. If Tinker Bell's light went out, she would die.

He searched all over the house, but he couldn't find anything that would help Tink. Suddenly, he had an idea. Peter stood up as tall as he could reach, his arms spread out wide.

"Boys and girls of the world!" he called. "Everyone who has ever dreamed of Neverland, please help Tinker Bell live! If you believe in Tinker Bell," he shouted, "clap your hands. Don't let Tink die!"

Peter waited. Then he heard a loud sound. It was far away, but soon it came closer and closer. At last Neverland was filled with the thunderous clapping of millions of children all over the world.

It worked! Tink's light grew brighter. Her voice grew strong. All at once, she leaped from the bed and flitted around the room! Fairy dust sparkled in the air!

Peter shouted his thanks to all the children who had helped Tinker Bell. "And now," he vowed, raising his sword, "to save the others."

Peter pressed through the dark, silent forest toward the bay. "It's Hook or me this time, I swear!" he shouted.

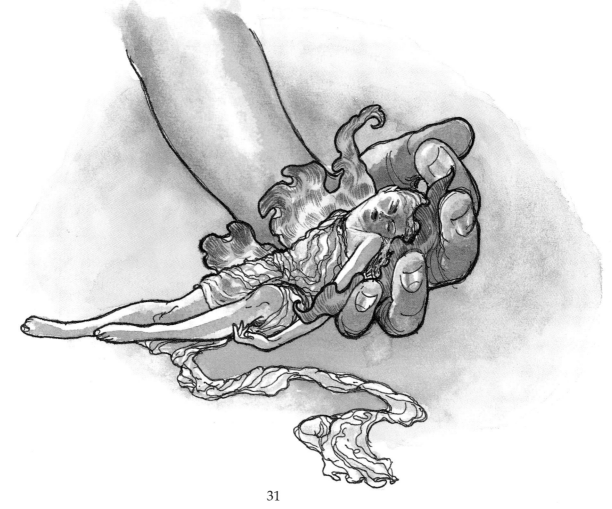

Captain Hook walked along the deck of his ship. He was happy. He had captured most of the Indians, and he had the three Darling children and all the Lost Boys.

"Ready the plank and bring the boys up from the brig!" he shouted to Smee.

The pirate did as he was told, and brought the boys up on deck. He bound their legs together with chains, locking them with a big brass lock.

"All right, boys," Hook said. "You can join me and my crew—or you can die. You first, John. What will it be?"

John drew himself up tall. "We'll not die. I say, Peter Pan will save us."

Hook let out a long, cruel laugh. "By this time," he told them, "Peter is lying dead, all alone in his great big bed."

"You liar!" Michael shouted. He tried to run to strike Hook, but the chain pulled tight around his legs. He fell to the deck with a thud.

Hook laughed again. He ordered John to walk the plank. John stood at the edge of the plank but would not walk on it. Hook grew angry.

"Bring up Wendy!" he shouted.

Smee and the pirates pulled Wendy up on deck. They tied her to the mast. Her shoulders began to shake.

Hook thought she must be cold. He decided to have a bit of fun and pretended to be kind. So he ordered one of the pirates to fetch his very own cape and cover Wendy so that she would be warm.

The boys tried to look brave for Wendy. But deep inside, they were scared.

"Now, boys, what will it be? Join me or walk the plank?
If you refuse to do either, you will see Wendy die first."
"No!" Michael screamed. The Lost Boys shook.
Wendy stood very still. "Be brave," she whispered.

Hook began to move toward Wendy. She took a deep breath. Michael and John gasped. Just as Hook reached Wendy, he heard a sound. *Tick-tick-tick-tick!*

Hook's eyes flashed open wide. His teeth began to chatter and his knees began to shake.

"The crocodile!" he shouted. "Hide me! Hide me!"

The pirates followed Hook down the gangway and deep into the hold of the ship. Within a few seconds, only the children were left on deck. The boys hopped to the side of the ship. They wanted to see the crocodile that had eaten Hook's hand.

The crocodile was not there. But Peter Pan was. He sprang out of hiding. Peter was making a wonderful ticking noise. The boys wanted to shout to him, but Peter stopped them.

"Quiet, boys," he said. "It's Hook or me this time. Don't spoil it now."

The boys moved back and waited for Peter's orders. Peter grabbed his sword. He climbed the side of the cabin and looked about. He could see a pirate coming toward him.

"Ready now," he whispered. "Here comes the first one."

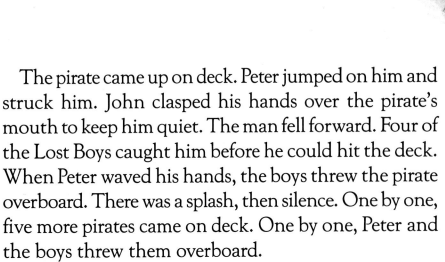

The pirate came up on deck. Peter jumped on him and struck him. John clasped his hands over the pirate's mouth to keep him quiet. The man fell forward. Four of the Lost Boys caught him before he could hit the deck. When Peter waved his hands, the boys threw the pirate overboard. There was a splash, then silence. One by one, five more pirates came on deck. One by one, Peter and the boys threw them overboard.

Soon, all was quiet. Peter slipped into Hook's cabin. Hook wasn't there. But Peter found a large brass key. He quietly crept on deck and opened the lock on the boys' chains. He signaled the boys to find any weapons they could, and to hide.

Peter sprang to Wendy's side. He took the cape off her shoulders and cut the ropes that held her. He quietly told her to hide with the boys. When she was safely hidden, Peter covered himself with the cape and stood leaning against the mast. Then he took a deep breath and crowed as loudly as his voice could yell.

"It's Peter Pan!" Hook screamed from down in the hold. The rest of the pirates rushed on deck. The deck was empty. Only the caped figure could be seen.

"Well, missy," one of the pirates said, "there's no one here but you now."

"There's one," the caped figure said.

"Who's that?"

"Peter Pan, the avenger!" came the answer. Peter flung off his cape. The pirates fell back in surprise. "Down and at them!" cried Peter to the boys.

In a moment, the ship was alive with the clash of swords. If the pirates had stayed together, they might have won. But they were not good fighters and they were afraid of Peter Pan. They ran here and there, letting themselves be easy targets for the boys. Some of the pirates jumped overboard into the sea. Some tried to hide in dark corners, but John and Michael found them.

At last, the fighting stopped. But suddenly, Captain Hook himself came rushing onto the deck. His long, sharp sword flashed in his one good hand. The boys surrounded him at once. Hook swung his sword at one boy after another. Each boy jumped back just in time to miss its edge.

Peter sprang into the middle of the fight. "This man is mine," he cried. Peter swung his own sword about his head. The boys stepped back to watch him fight.

Hook now stood face to face with Peter. Peter's eyes narrowed. He swung his sword slowly from side to side. Hook sneered and let loose his meanest laugh. Suddenly, he jabbed at Peter, but Peter jumped out of the way and flew to another part of the deck.

Hook was angry. "Stay put!" he shouted.

Now it was Peter's turn to laugh. He leaped down onto the deck, throwing Hook off balance. But Hook spun around and swung at Peter. Their swords clashed. The sound of metal hitting metal rang loudly in the air. Peter laughed again, then swung his sword again at Hook. On and on they fought, each poking and jabbing and swinging his sword at the other.

Once more Peter lunged at Hook, this time knocking the sword from Hook's hand. Peter smiled.

"So, Hook. At last I have you at my mercy."

Peter bowed low, kicked the sword close to Hook, and told him to pick it up. Hook sprang for the weapon, and the battle was on again.

"I am youth. I am joy," Peter cried.

Hook fought as hard as he could. But Peter fluttered around him and always stayed just outside his reach. Again and again, Peter darted in and pricked Hook's arm or his leg. Hook knew that he could not fight much longer. Then Peter raised his sword and jumped through the air at Hook.

Hook sprang to the bulwarks. "You won't have me today!" he shouted.

Suddenly, Hook leaped overboard into the sea. There was a splashing and thrashing noise next to the ship. Hook screamed, then all was silent. In a moment, a soft *tick-tick-tick-tick* could be heard swimming away from the ship.

"So," Peter said, "the crocodile has finally eaten all of Captain James Hook." John, Michael, the Lost Boys, and Wendy gathered around Peter, cheering.

"All right," he said. "The ship is ours. Turn her about and head for home!"

The night was very still in the Darling home. It was close to the end of summer, and there was a slight chill in the air. Mr. Darling thought there was a draft coming from the children's bedroom. He went into the room to close the window. But Mrs. Darling stopped him. She wanted the window to stay open. It reminded her of her children before they had disappeared.

Mrs. Darling looked around the room. She had come into the bedroom again and again, hoping to see her three children back in their beds. But each time, she found the beds empty. She sat down on Wendy's bed and breathed a sigh. Mr. Darling sat down next to her. He put his arm around her to make her feel better. Their dog, Nana, walked slowly into the room. Her head was bent down. She also missed the children.

Mr. and Mrs. Darling still did not know what had happened to their children. The last time they saw Wendy, John, and Michael was just before leaving for the party. All three were sound asleep in their beds. When Mr. and Mrs. Darling returned, their children were gone.

Nana had tried to tell them that Wendy, John, and Michael flew away into the night. But dogs couldn't talk. And children couldn't fly, or so Mr. and Mrs. Darling believed.

"All we can do is wait and hope," Mr. Darling said.

"Yes," Mrs. Darling said with a sad voice. "Wait, hope, and keep the window open."

They sat together for a long time. They were both thinking of the children. Finally, they grew tired. It was time to go to bed. Mr. and Mrs. Darling stood up slowly. "Come, Nana," Mrs. Darling said. "No sense waiting in here tonight."

Nana rose sadly and followed the Darlings out of the room.

"Quick," Peter said as he and Tinker Bell dropped to the floor through the open window. "I thought they would never leave. Come on now, Tink. Help me close the window. When Wendy arrives, she will see the window closed and locked. She will think that her mother and father have closed her out. Then she will lead the boys back to Neverland and stay with us forever."

Peter and Tinker Bell had a hard time pushing the window closed. It had remained open so long that some of the hinges had become stuck. Peter heard Nana bark.

"Quick, Tink. The big dog is coming back!"

Peter and Tinker Bell pushed as hard as they could. At last, the window moved. Peter and Tink flew out the window, then shut it tight from the outside.

Nana came bouncing and barking to the room. Mrs. Darling ran in after her. At once, she rushed over to the window and opened it. She thought the window must have closed by itself, although she could not think of how that could have happened. She tied the window back with heavy rope so that it would not close again.

Peter saw her sit on John's bed. Very soon, he saw two tears roll down her cheeks. She bent down and laid her head on her arms.

"She's crying," Peter said. "She really does love her children. She wants them to come home."

Tinker Bell shook her bells sadly.

"Come on, Tink. Let's go away from the window." And so they flew away, over the roof and out of sight.

At last, Mr. Darling came into the bedroom. He turned out the lights and led Mrs. Darling and Nana back to their own beds.

Many hours passed. The house was quiet. But just before daybreak, Wendy, John and Michael flew through the bedroom window. They were tired from their long flight. They wondered why Tinker Bell had left them before they were halfway across the sea. Still, they were very excited to be home at last. Wendy heard Nana barking downstairs in the kitchen.

"She is bound to wake everyone up," Wendy told the boys. "Let's surprise Mother and Father. Hurry, get into your beds." Wendy also jumped into her bed and dove under the covers.

Nana came running back into the room. She jumped and barked and filled the house with noise. Mr. and Mrs. Darling came dashing in to see what all of Nana's noise was about.

Wendy jumped out of bed. "Mother! Father!" she cried.

"It's Wendy!" Mother screamed. At first she thought it was a dream.

John jumped up. "Hello, everyone. It's fun to be back."

"It's John!" Father cried, but he could hardly believe his eyes.

Nana rushed over to Michael's bed and pulled the covers back. She began to bark wildly.

"It's me!" Michael shouted.

They all stretched their arms out wide and ran to each other. They hugged and kissed until they were all too tired to hold onto each other anymore. All the while, Peter Pan and Tinker Bell went unnoticed. They were outside the window, looking in.

"Oh, Mother, Father," Wendy said when she could catch her breath at last, "we have such news to tell you!"

"Yes, yes," John and Michael said. "We have been to Neverland. We have lived with Peter Pan and Tinker Bell and the Lost Boys. We have seen Indians and fought with pirates!"

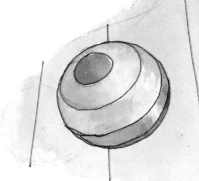

"Yes," said Wendy. "We saw mermaids and whales too. And we met the lovely Indian Princess, Tiger Lily."

Mr. and Mrs. Darling could hardly believe all they were hearing. "Who are the Lost Boys?" they asked.

"Oh, goodness," Wendy said and ran to the door. "I almost forgot. They are boys who live in Neverland. Their home is in a big hole under the ground."

"They all sleep in one bed, and they have mushrooms for chairs," Michael said.

"And we have brought them home with us," John said excitedly.

Mr. and Mrs. Darling stared at the children. "But their parents will worry about them."

"They have no mother and father," Wendy said.

"Humph," said Peter, who was still looking in at the window. "They have me!"

Mr. Darling looked at his wife. "Well," he said slowly, "six more children will be a lot of children."

Mrs. Darling smiled. "Yes, I know. But come on, let's go and meet them."

The Darling children cheered. John and Michael rushed out of the room. They each wanted to be the first to tell the Lost Boys that they were going to stay and live with the Darling family forever.

Suddenly, Wendy heard a tap at the window. Not until Nana and her parents had left the room did she go to the window and look out.

"Hello, Peter. Hello, Tinker Bell. I wondered what happened to you. Will you two come and live with us?"

Peter shook his head. "No," he said. "I never want to grow up. I want to live in Neverland and have fun."

"Oh," Wendy said sadly, "then you have come to say good bye." She found it hard to say goodbye to Peter.

"Don't forget me," Peter said.

"I'll never forget you, Peter," said Wendy. Tears filled her eyes. "The window will always be open for you."

Peter Pan smiled and waved goodbye. Tinker Bell shook her tiny bells in farewell. Fairy dust fell as she did. Wendy watched until they were completely out of sight. Then she went downstairs to join her family, leaving the window open behind her.

47